the little things:

love and heartbreak

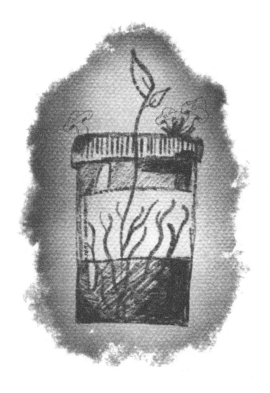

Devan Woods

the little things:

love and heartbreak

the fear of your own mind.

the fear of your own thoughts and
emotions.

they're so quiet until they're
ringing in your head.

the silence breaks.

- devan woods

only thing

the pitter-patter of the heart,

the all-day restlessness,

the overall preoccupation that goes

along with experiencing love.

it hurts to feel the pull at my heart.

it hurts to know i overthink.

what hurts the most is that you're the

only thing i can think about.

you

i miss you.

i miss your voice.

your hair.

your eyes.

your hugs.

your laugh.

i miss everything about you.

that night

traveling the same roads that you took

me on back on the night that we met.

i replay the songs that you sang to me as

we were riding.

when you dropped me off,

you have me a hug.

my heart just stopped.

for a minute i thought i was lost,

because i never had felt this way before.

when you picked me up the next day

i felt like i knew what to say.

the words disappeared,

but when i saw you,

my whole world reappeared.

dear you,

i want to know you and to grow with you.

i want to meet your friends and family,

but i want to meet everything about you

as well.

i ease my way into my own thoughts just

thinking of you.

my thoughts scare me because of my

fears.

i fear i could never be loved by you,

because i'm only here to help others be

loved.

i fear that i push myself towards you too

much, and that i'm just a bother.

i fear that these fears get the best of me

when thinking of you,

but at the same time, i have no fear of
you.
it's the thoughts of you that my mind
makes up.
i fear that i talk too much or show too
much joy.
i fear that when we say "goodbye" you
leave relieved.
i fear that when we say "goodnight" it has
no meaning.
and i fear that when i miss you, it's just
me.

expectations

i can't expect you to treat us like we're in a
relationship.
we aren't in a relationship,
so, i get it,
but little emotions go a long way for me.
i pay attention to every little thing about
you.
i understand that you still want to be closed
off to yourself,
but it hurts.

it hurts not knowing if you're alright or if you
care to talk to me about your problems.
i sit and wonder what i must do to show that
i truly care,
but you seem so strong headed that i can't
get it through your mind.
it hurts to not know what's happening
because you're so closed off,
and it hurts to know that this might all be
one sided.

nowadays

The heart, a fortress, once laid bare,

Now shielded, with walls of despair.

A melody once danced upon his lips,

Now silenced by bitter, love's eclipse.

The wounds of affection, too deep to
heal,

Scorched by love's flame, too raw to
conceal.

is it you?

what is this?

what are we?

every time i see you, i want to wrap my

arms around you and hug you,

but i don't know who else you hug.

i want to grab your face and kiss you,

but i don't know who else you'd been

kissing.

i want to call you at night and tell you

how much i love you,

but i don't know who else you call.

i want to have you in my bed every night,

but i don't know who else thinks the

same.

self-judgment

it's a struggle to be myself every day.

i go to put eyeshadow on,

but i get disgusted by myself.

men shouldn't wear makeup i say to myself,

so, i wipe it off.

i cry myself to sleep.

there are points where i love to wear
eyeliner because it shows artistic skills and
creativity with colors,

but in my mind, it's just another judgment.

i put another layer of being "different" on
top of a man who still isn't safe within
himself.

some days i feel like i'm stranded on in place

where i have all the freedom to be who i

want,

but it's my mind that has control.

fix it.

growing up with thinking i was gay i was always "the fixer" because it was easier to focus on others' issues and fix their problems rather than my own.

so many people would say "i feel like i can tell you anything" or "you're so easy to talk to", but i feel like the reason i was so good at being there for other people was because deep down i needed that kind of person there for me.

life has passed by and looking back i was everything for those people. everything to them when i wasn't everything to myself.

i always listened to everyone else's problems and could never feel comfortable with telling them my problems or feelings because i didn't know if i could trust them with me opening up.

they were never asking anyways.

they all thought i was a solid rock that was perfectly okay, but in all reality, i was truly a mess.

i knew in my own mind i was different but denied it and tried to cover it up with being like the other people who were "perfect."

nobody knew what i was going through, and i don't understand how i hid it so well.

little boy

you tried to tell me who i was.

little boys don't play with barbie dolls.

woke up one morning and thought,

i want to try that leopard dress on.

you made me feel like i was drowning.

at such a young age i was surrounded

by words that hurt me and tore me

down.

how could i face the world now?

little boy it will be alright.

keep your head up and loosen your

shoulders.

don't worry about the shirt you have on.

it might feel tight but that's just the way

the world works.

these people are going to try to bring

you down.

such a young age they know you'll easily

frown.

fantasies

is my mind making up a male fantasy?

the creation of you

or who i want you to be.

a simple i miss you can go a long way,

but when the time comes it's only a

phrase.

i think of you every day, awaiting you

calls like child's play.

is he missing me like i'm missing him?

brick walls

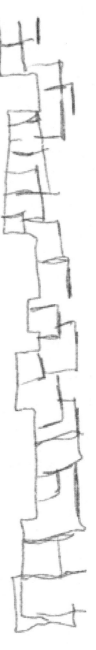

it's hard to stop myself.

it's hard to not think about you.

it's hard to not text you and just see how

you are.

it's hard not to miss you.

your eyes, your smile, your laugh.

everything about you.

it hurts to feel like you don't care slightly

enough.

it hurts to sit here and think "if i don't

text will he even care?"

i fear

i don't think you could ever love me.

i was taught to radiate and receive,

but i feel like you've received all my

radiation that you're just soaking it up

without having a thought.

i want to love you,

but i have nothing left to radiate.

not even love for myself.

this is one of my main fears.

i tend to love people too much and care

to the point that i lose myself in loving

other people.

i fear that i scare you away.

i fear that i make you hate me.

lips

craving the feeling of your lips pressed

against mine.

feeling the warmth from your breath,

the whispers from your mouth,

the softness of your lips imagined.

comfort found within the thought.

pain healed by the simple touch of just

this.

your lips

•••

you say it was nothing and that we were
just friends,
but friends don't treat friends the way
you treated me.
was it because i was there,
and you took advantage of it?
was i the only one you could text
"i love you" to because i was the only
one putting any effort into making you
feel loved?
was it because i was in-front of you, and
you just wanted to show someone you
can love?

was it that you knew all along i'd fall so in

love with you to the point you didn't

want anything because you can't love

yourself like i loved you?

too early

cover up your cuts with band aids.

hide away your pain and fears.

little boy it'll be okay.

you don't have to hide your tears.

p.b.

pretty boy,

i love you.

i love your soft black hair and everything

about you.

when i hear your voice,

i start to miss you,

but i know this feeling might be quite an

issue.

when i think of you,

i think of happy endings.

like maybe a wedding day,

or adopting many babies.

neverland

i used to wish i could fly,

to the second star on the right.

taking me straight on to morning

where i wouldn't have to hide.

ttyl

i deserved a better goodbye.

i deserved to know why you made me

feel the way you did,

but then abandoned me out of nowhere.

to know why you made me feel like i was

in love just to be told it was nothing.

to feel so sure about you and to have felt

so safe,

only to fear and hate.

to understand why i put so much

thought and care into love,

only for you to strike it away.

Here

i want you here.

i want to brush my fingers through your
hair as you lay your head on my lap one
last time.

i want to feel the feeling again of
knowing you'll hug me before you leave.

i want to see your notifications and to
feel the butterfly feeling one last time.

as much as i shouldn't be saying all of
this...

i wish i had you here.

sweater weather

the temperature is changing,
the wind is howling,
my body is shivering.
i should be enjoying the fall weather...
but i can't.
i can't when i'm shaking thinking about you.
tears flood out.
feeling faint as i imagine your eyes.
the constant phrase "i miss him" being on my
mind...
i go to say it out loud,
but i can't.
i've come too far.
i've grown without you for too long now.
you don't deserve it.
friends don't do what you did,
and someone who loves you shouldn't show
how a heart should hurt.

masterpiece

i'm just another art piece,

another picture hanging on your wall,

a picture sitting painted so beautifully,

just waiting to admire your eyes,

waiting to admire you,

but mainly waiting for you to admire me.

pillows

i had a few dreams about-
you and i

usually when i dream, they come right to
life

i had a couple bout you
that stuck like glue,
and they're playing in the back of my
mind

i wish you knew-
the pain you drew-
like a dagger falling from the sky.

i wish you'd take a glimpse
of what you'd miss

happy thoughts

remember when you said you love how
you can make me smile?

i miss it.

i miss laughing because of you.

ivy

my thoughts spread like poison ivy

it hurts to hold in the pain of not

scratching at it

but i must keep the pain

so it doesn't spread and cover all of me

i wait patiently hoping i get the guts to

scratch it open

it hurts so much that i try to nudge it

so it grows

farther and farther

more and more

it's covering my heart with so much pain

but i try to scratch it open

you left once i did

i've had poison ivy ever since

ball

it's a ball of nothing but fuzz.

a mess of mixtures.

the colors are all mixed in

red,

blue,

and purple.

red for the anger and hate,

blue for the sadness and pain,

purple for the discomfort of self.

this ball bounces itself around.

each bounce picks up a new fuzz ball,

but it's a ball of nothing but trust...

trust thrown all around.

timing

too many times,

i've fallen for someone who only loves
me in the dark.

it's not quite right,

they say after months of leading me on.

maybe it's me.

i'm just not so deserving of love.

love

icarus was the boy who flew too close to
the sun. me?

i'm the boy who flew too close to love,
the boy who thought so much of love,
the boy who stated that love was real,
the boy who shortly found out that love
wasn't real to himself anymore.
proven that love can be painful,
proven that love can be one sided,
proven that love can make one of the
happiest and most loving people fall into
so many pieces with nobody there to put
them back together.

icarus was the boy who flew too close to
the sun,

and i was the boy who grew to hate love.

elegy

our love, an elegy, both soft and frail,

an unspoken verse, a fading tale.

emotions penned in ink so pure,

lost in the abyss of love unsure.

your touch, a memory i cling to tight,

in the symphony of a lonely night.

our love, an elegy i softly weep,

a requiem for a love so deep.

whispers

dreams shattered like shards of glass,

a love story that couldn't amass.

promises whispered in the night,

now shattered remnants in my sight.

love's canvas painted in hues of pain,

a masterpiece washed in the rain.

your departure, a bleak sunrise,

mourning the love that met demise.

Made in United States
North Haven, CT
14 May 2024

52499728R00054